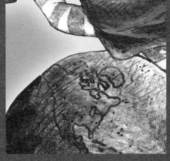

The Park
Our Town Built

Written by
Diane Gonzales Bertrand

Illustrated by
Tania Bauerle

For Renée, Barry, Matthew,
and Kyle, with love.
- Diane

For my shining stars –
Kevin, Isabelle, and Zoe.
- Tanja

©2011 Raven Tree Press

All rights reserved. For information about permission to
reproduce selections from this book, write to: Permissions,
Raven Tree Press, a Division of Delta Systems Co., Inc.,
1400 Miller Parkway, McHenry, IL 60050 www.raventreepress.com

Bertrand, Diane Gonzales.

The Park Our Town Built / written by Diane Gonzales Bertrand:
illustrated by Tanja Bauerle; —1 ed. — McHenry, IL ; Raven Tree
Press, 2011.

p. cm.

SUMMARY: In this cumulative story, townspeople work together
to build a park and then celebrate their achievement with fireworks
and a party.

English Edition
ISBN 978-1-936299-14-0 hardcover
Bilingual Edition
ISBN 978-1-936299-12-6 hardcover

Audience: pre–K to 3rd grade.
Title available in English-only or bilingual English-Spanish
(concept words only) editions.

1. Parks--Fiction. 2. City and town life--Fiction.
3. Words/Concepts--Fiction I. Bauerle, Tanja, 1970- ill.
II. Title.

Library of Congress Control Number: 2010936676

Printed in Taiwan
10 9 8 7 6 5 4 3 2 1
First Edition

**Free activities for this book are available at
www.raventreepress.com**

PRINTED WITH
SOY INK

Raven Tree Press
A Division of Delta Systems Co., Inc.
www.raventreepress.com

This is the park our town built.

This is the man

who gave us the land

for the park our town built.

This is the mayor

who spoke to the man
who gave us the land
for the park our town built.

These are the children

who went with the mayor
who spoke to the man
who gave us the land
for the park our town built.

These are the people

who helped the children
who went with the mayor
who spoke to the man
who gave us the land
for the park our town built.

These are the tools

carried by the people
who helped the children
who went with the mayor
who spoke to the man
who gave us the land
for the park our town built.

These are the swings

made with the tools
carried by the people
who helped the children
who went with the mayor
who spoke to the man
who gave us the land
for the park our town built.

This is the slide

that matches the swings
made with the tools
carried by the people
who helped the children
who went with the mayor
who spoke to the man
who gave us the land
for the park our town built.

This is the bridge

built near the slide
that matches the swings
made with the tools
carried by the people
who helped the children
who went with the mayor
who spoke to the man
who gave us the land
for the park our town built.

This is the fountain

20

behind the bridge
built near the slide
that matches the swings
made with the tools
carried by the people
who helped the children
who went with the mayor
who spoke to the man
who gave us the land
for the park our town built.

These are the benches

that circle the fountain
behind the bridge
built near the slide
that matches the swings
made with the tools
carried by the people
who helped the children
who went with the mayor
who spoke to the man
who gave us the land
for the park our town built.

This is the garden

that grows near the benches
that circle the fountain
behind the bridge
built near the slide
that matches the swings
made with the tools
carried by the people
who helped the children
who went with the mayor
who spoke to the man
who gave us the land
for the park our town built.

These are the families

who planted the garden
that grows near the benches
that circle the fountain
behind the bridge
built near the slide
that matches the swings
made with the tools
carried by the people
who helped the children
who went with the mayor
who spoke to the man
who gave us the land
for the park our town built.

This is the party

for all of the families
who planted the garden
that grows near the benches
that circle the fountain
behind the bridge
built near the slide
that matches the swings
made with the tools
carried by the people
who helped the children
who went with the mayor
who spoke to the man
who gave us the land
for the park our town built.

29

These are the fireworks

that go off at the party
for all of the families
who planted the garden
that grows near the benches
that circle the fountain
behind the bridge
built near the slide
that matches the swings
made with the tools
carried by the people
who helped the children
who went with the mayor
who spoke to the man
who gave us the land
for the park our town built.

 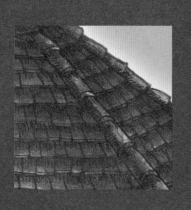  
   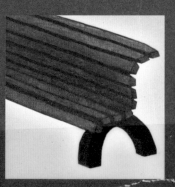